A TINY HOUSE CHRISTMAS

A RUNAWAY BRIDE CHRISTMAS ROMANCE

HOCKEY SWEETHEARTS

JEAN ORAM

A Tiny House Christmas

A Runaway Bride Christmas Romance

A Hockey Sweethearts Novella
By Jean Oram

© 2023, 2024 Jean Oram
All rights reserved
Second Edition
(extended)

Printed in the United States of America unless otherwise stated on the last page of this book. Published by Oram Productions Alberta, Canada.

COMPLETE LIBRARY OF CONGRESS CATALOGING-IN-PUBLICATION DATA AVAILABLE ONLINE

Oram, Jean.

A Tiny House Christmas / Jean Oram.—2nd. ed.

ISBN: 978-1-990833-97-7, 978-1-990833-98-4 (paperback) 978-1-990833-99-1, 978-1-990833-96-0 (large print), 9781990833878 (ebook)

First Oram Productions Edition: April 2025

Front cover design by Jess Mastorakos

AN AUTHOR'S NOTE

I had SO much fun writing Karlene's runaway bride story. When I started the Hockey Sweethearts series she was always sort of in the back of my mind as a character I might like to write about as some sort of bonus book. Then when I was writing Sugar Cookie Country House in 2023—a book that took me *so* incredibly long—I started to get more and more curious about Karlene. Suddenly she was a runaway bride. Who knew?

At one point I even set Sugar Cookie aside for a few days in July and wrote the first draft of Karlene's story because it was *just there* in my mind and I didn't want to lose it. The first draft just *flowed*. I LOVED the idea of her running away from her wedding. Add in a little age gap between her and the man she loves, a secret crush, a brother's best friend, a cowboy, a ranch… Oh, it was *fun*!

I hope this bonus novella is as much fun to read as it was to write.

XO,

Jean Oram

A Tiny House Christmas

CHAPTER 1

DECEMBER 23

He was Joe McCall to everyone who knew him. Except to Karlene.

His best friend's kid sister was the only one who still called him Joey—and the only one allowed to without facing dire consequences.

If Karlene ever called him Joe, he knew she was mad—as mad as the time she'd shown up at seventeen, as angry as the thunderstorm gathering around the ranch, wanting to ride off her fight with her then-boyfriend-now-fiancé Thomas. Joey had refused to let her ride his stallion out into the storm, and he'd been called Joe that day.

The next month she'd bought her own horse. Which, naturally, he'd allowed her to board, free of charge, on his ranch ever since.

There were a few other rare times she'd called him Joe. For instance, the occasions he'd sided with her older brother Blake and said no to her tagging along on their adventures. He'd like to think he'd made up for that with a few secrets and favors over the years. For example, Blake didn't know about the old cabin he and Karlene had found a few miles ride from his ranch, a place they'd camp out in a few times a season.

Karlene called him Joey at least ninety-nine percent of the time, which he figured was a decent ratio for a cowboy and his best friend's kid sister.

He shook his head, taking in the line of six bridesmaids standing to his right. Karlene had a way about her, that was for sure. He still hadn't figured out how she'd convinced him to be one of her bridesmaids. Or a dude of honor, or whatever she called it to make him feel better about it all.

Who could say no to her when her eyes lit up whenever she stepped onto his ranch, and that bounce fell into her booted step? You'd have to be some kind of monster to shoo her away.

And so here he was in spiffy dark-washed jeans, a tuxedo jacket and a fresh new cowboy hat that matched the men to his left, waiting for Karlene to come down the aisle. It was two days before Christmas and the Sweetheart Creek church was decorated in red and green for the seasonal wedding and all of the pews were packed. A wave of pride filled him, dampening his eyes as Karlene appeared in the church doorway in her white gown. Six years his junior, the tagalong kid had grown up on him. Today she was a bride, about to get married.

Married.

Little Karlene Spragg.

A wife. It was going to change everything.

He supposed it was about time, though. She was pushing thirty-years-old and had been dating Thomas McNaughton since high school. And yet, somehow, the fact that she was all grown up hadn't registered with Joey. Not even when he'd been drawn into the wedding party, all the plans thankfully taken care of by Thomas's mother, leaving him out of decisions regarding floral arrangements, color schemes and nail polish.

Maybe today didn't feel real because Kar hadn't ever truly had her heart broken, or been wrung out on the adult dating scene like he had. And now she was going to be a wife to a man outside his social circle.

Her husband-to-be's family had one of the biggest ranches in Hill Country, and next week Karlene would no doubt move her horse—which was currently rigged up to the carriage out front, ready to take her and Thomas from the church to the wedding reception—to her own ranch.

Hers and Thomas'.

She'd have kids. Quit her job as a physical therapist for the NHL hockey team in San Antonio and become so busy he'd rarely see her. She'd no longer need him after today, and a stab of loneliness ached in his gut.

He rolled onto the balls of his feet, fighting the sense of loss. He met Karlene's eyes across the church and the air left his lungs.

Somewhere along the line, her familiar legginess had made her a knockout without him noticing. She was simply stunning, the dress hugging her curves.

He bounced in place again. Something felt right about waiting for her to walk down the aisle toward him.

He frowned at the fleeting thought, then became distracted by how Karlene was frozen in the church doorway like his prize bull had gotten out again and she was afraid of becoming a target.

Karlene's round eyes locked on Joey's and the hitch in her shoulders dropped. His gut warmed and he caught himself taking a half step forward before catching himself. The heat spread as memories of this woman, his best friend, flooded through him. Laughter. Horseback rides and camp-outs at their secret cabin. The two of them cooking breakfast in his kitchen after an endless night of calving cows, elbow to elbow.

He reminded himself that she wasn't here for him. And this wasn't the day or time to swoop in and look out for her. That was over now. She had other people to do that.

Karlene Spragg and her long legs were all grown up.

But his gut told him she wasn't okay.

She needed something. A friend. Him.

She was wavering in the doorway, seemingly unable to move down the aisle.

Was she waiting for something from *him*?

He almost stepped forward again.

What was she asking him?

He waited, trying to read her mind, predict her needs.

Did she feel...?

His breath left him.

Did he...?

He blinked, wondering when his feelings had shifted for this woman who fit into his life like she'd been made for it.

His Karlene.

She still wasn't moving down the aisle, questions lingering in her eyes.

Should she?

Did he feel...?

Could they...?

He gave a slight nod, letting her know that he was here. He was always here.

And that somehow he'd fallen in love with her.

Now that it was too late.

* * *

Karlene had chosen her wedding song a long time ago, back when she'd been full of fantasies and crushing on a man six years her senior.

This song was her one thumbprint on today.

She wavered at the church's threshold, trying to catch her breath so she could savor this awaited moment, feel the excitement, will the music to carry her down the aisle.

Her best friend Joey was in the large wedding party lineup and as she maintained eye contact with him, the tension eased.

Steady, steady Joey. It would all be okay if he was here, at her side.

In a few short moments she was going to be a rancher's wife. She was going to live in the country with horses, just like he did.

It had barely taken any thought or planning to find herself here today—in a church packed to the rafters with expectant friends and family members. And at the front, waited Thomas in a black cowboy hat, boots, and a tuxedo with Western flares to suit his rancher style.

Joey was still looking at her and she smoothed a trembling hand over the dress her future mother-in-law had chosen. Joey was worried. She needed to smile. To unfreeze herself and walk down the aisle and seize her future. Make her scrapbook, which was tattered and worn, into a photo album instead of a wish book.

In minutes, she'd have a handsome cowboy husband.

A ranch filled with horses.

Her place to belong where life was paced by the seasons and the animals around her.

Just like she'd always dreamed.

She smiled, lifted her left foot, still hovering on the threshold.

Her supporting leg wobbled, and Joey leaned forward as though about to step out of the bridesmaids' line.

She tried to put her left foot down, but her body refused to move forward. She raised a finger as if to say to those watching, "One moment." Sweat gathered under the tightness of her dress.

She could feel the guests' eyes on her, the pews packed shoulder to shoulder, smiles turning amused as she faltered.

Her eyes stayed locked on Joey's and that foreign look he was giving her.

She knew he understood her.

But this look in his gaze. It was new.

It was as though he *saw* her today.

Her as an adult woman, and not a tagalong kid.

She blinked long and hard. She'd gotten over her crush years ago—she'd forced herself to when Thomas had begun questioning her about the amount of time she spent on Joey's ranch.

We're just friends.

He sees me as a tagalong. Blake's kid sister.

Nothing more.

But the way Joey was taking her in with those expressive, sweet eyes of his was unnerving. There was a new warmth and depth. And it was exactly what she'd always wanted to see reflected back at her.

She tried to look away. She needed to move down the aisle. Say I do.

But then Joey gave her a tiny nod, so small nobody else would notice the way he was giving her permission.

Her breathing eased and her foot landed on the floor.

Permission to be herself. To follow her heart.

To *run*.

Before she could process her own thoughts, Karlene had spun around and was sprinting outside and down the church's steps. Her fingers shaky, she muttered "hurry, hurry" as she unhitched her horse, Becky, from the carriage out front.

She freed the mare, gathering the long reins meant to reach the carriage driver as she pulled the horse closer to the carriage. One high heel planted on its step and, with the sound of her gown tearing underfoot, she threw herself onto Becky's waiting back.

"Cha!" she hollered, her heart hammering as she squeezed her knees, sending the startled mare forward as members of the wedding party flooded the parking area.

She was pretty sure she heard her mother scream "Karlene Abigail Spragg, you get back here right this instant or I'll tan your hide!" before the sounds of her mare's hooves at full gallop drowned out everything but the sound of Karlene's beating heart.

* * *

Inflatable Christmas decorations waved as Karlene and the horse veered across a snowless Texas lawn, short-cutting through a backyard. Karlene tucked herself low as the mare flew over a falling-down split-rail fence at the edge of town, praying she wouldn't slide off its bare back.

The horse landed and continued across the open pasture.

Freedom.

She headed north, splashing through the creek the town of Sweetheart Creek was named after, then up its banks, the land unfolding around her; the houses shrinking behind her. She urged Becky faster, checking again to see if anyone had taken Thomas's horse and was following her.

Not a soul.

To her right, several hundred feet away, there was a vehicle on the adjacent gravel road, dust clouding out behind it. She veered left, crossing the highway and moving northeast.

The December air was cold, whistling through her wedding gown. The skirt flopped against the horse's flanks, billowing and crashing, at the mercy of her speed and the wind.

Karlene rode as hard as she dared, skirting fences that delineated properties, avoiding roads and anywhere a truck could catch up with her. She just needed to be away. Away from the church. Away from the expectations that had suddenly made her feel as though she was struggling under water, unable to breathe.

Thomas McNaughton was nearly every woman's Mr. Right. He was handsome, kind, and had a giant ranch with a long, rich legacy that made her parents' light up whenever it was mentioned. And it was mentioned an eye-rolling amount. As agricultural researchers for a local college, they wanted access to one of Texas's largest cattle ranches, and the McNaughtons wanted a hardworking bride for Thomas. Someone who'd help him build and continue the family legacy. Thomas, in so many ways, *was* the legacy.

At first, it had been fun, and she'd felt important by association.

But Karlene had learned over the years that there were some heavy expectations in regards to how she'd fit into their ranch, and that her suggestions would be politely disregarded, unlike on Joey's ranch. The McNaughtons expected her to quit her job immediately after the wedding. Give up her career as the physical therapist for the San Antonio's National Hockey League team, the Dragons, and focus on creating the next generation of McNaughtons.

Her parents expectations were simple—grease the wheels with her family-to-be and make sure the planned research project went off without a hitch.

But as the wedding plans had unrolled, Karlene had realized that none of it was about her. It was about the ranch. And, even if she loved Tom and he loved her, she'd never be more than a supporting character.

But she'd stuck with it all because being with Tom on his ranch was all so incredibly close to the future she'd envisioned for herself as a kid on her grandparent's own ranch.

So close.

She swiped at her tears, wishing she could go back in time and somehow fix it all. Maybe if she'd stood up for herself, or asked Tom for more say in how things were run, or even just insisted on planning her own wedding. Something. Anything.

Instead, she'd stayed quiet and now she was hurting Tom by running away, leaving him standing in the church.

She'd almost had it all, and now it was surely ruined.

All of it.

But it would have been ruined either way. If she'd stood up for herself it would have only led to fights and Tom feeling as though he had to take sides in an impossible situation.

And yet, it would have been better than doing the most mortifying and embarrassing thing in her life so far—running away from her wedding and humiliating her fiancé.

She swiped at her cheeks, almost toppling off Becky, letting her slow to a canter.

Standing in the church, feeling the warmth coming from Joey, she'd known. She'd known that no matter how hard she tried, she wouldn't have that spark she'd dreamed of having with her future husband. Fighting harder wouldn't have created easy laughter and routines that evolved without discussion. There'd always be steady involvement from his parents. In their eyes, there was too much at stake to entrust the ranch to the next generation, or even to an outsider like herself.

She'd chosen a good man in Thomas, but the wrong man. And she'd lacked the courage to tell herself that before putting on this dress.

Becky slowed to a walking pace and Karlene lifted her face to the late afternoon sky, pale blue already shifting into darker tones. Less than an hour before dusk. Night would fall quickly, as would the temperature. She needed a plan.

She squared her shoulders and inhaled the expansive Texas sky. Even bigger than the beautiful land at her feet. Always there like Joey.

Karlene checked the horizon out of habit and spotted a horse coming straight for them at full gallop from an eastern angle. It was not someone from the church. The figure was bigger than her fiancé. For a moment her breath caught and her imagination played a trick. The rider looked like her late grandfather, and a familiar feeling of love expanded in her chest as she watched how he rode with ease, as though he and the horse were one.

She shook off the feeling and tried to coax Becky into a trot, but the mare huffed and refused. The other rider was angling to cut her off, his horse fresher, the cowboy seated squarely in a saddle.

There was no avoiding it. She was caught.

Tears of frustration welled in her eyes. She wasn't ready to explain herself, or to be guilted into returning to the church. And she definitely wasn't ready to face the small town rumors and hubbub that was surely building around her sudden departure.

"Karlene!"

She urged her tired horse faster, steering away from the approaching rider. Her inner thighs and seat were already sore from the abuse of riding bareback.

She sighed, defeated, as the sound of hooves tearing up the pasture grew louder. She turned Becky, ready to face her opponent. She squinted against the setting sun, then shielded her eyes as the cowboy drew up alongside her.

It was Joey. And there was no heat in his gaze. No invitation.

Just concern for tagalong kid Karlene.

"Why did you nod at me?" she snapped. If it weren't for him, she'd be in that church, marrying the man she loved right now. She'd have found a way down that aisle. She'd have found a way to make the dream work, and she'd have what she wanted.

She swiped at her eyes. She was such a fool where Joey McCall was concerned. He'd probably only meant to be encouraging, and she'd thought...

She shook her head at herself. He hadn't been asking her to choose him, and yet...she had done just that.

And now she could see that she had, in fact, chosen absolutely nothing.

* * *

"How did you know where to find me?" Karlene snapped, her tone tight. "Who sent you here, Joe?"

Joey pulled back on the reins, controling his dancing horse. "Nobody."

And as for how he'd found her, he'd just known. It was like in the mornings when he stepped out on his porch and knew whether it was going to rain.

After Karlene had left the church doorway, the room had been still for a long, heavy beat. Then he'd found himself jogging down the empty aisle. Ahead of Thomas, ahead of her family.

Once he'd reached the church's outer door, and seeing her free Becky from the carriage, he'd stopped cold, forcing traffic to jam up behind him, giving her the gift of time. Not that she'd needed it. She'd been impressively fast, as though she was ranked the world champion of runaway brides.

Karlene had been away before her mom could even finish her impromptu scolding.

Then Joey had been in his truck, burning up the road, lurching to a halt in front of his barn. He'd saddled his horse, Cavalcade, grabbed the star bag he kept fully stocked and at the ready for longer rides. Then, recalling what Karlene was wearing, ran inside and scooped up a change of clothes. He'd been off, angling toward the distant town without even thinking how impossible it could be to find Karlene.

But now that he had, he held his horse alongside hers, his stallion's nostrils flaring from the brisk ride's exertion.

Karlene was taking in their surroundings, as though only just realizing how far she'd ridden from town, and how she'd drifted to a familiar trail they'd blazed a dozen times to the old cabin in the hills. The log building had once been used by cowboys to stay in while looking over calving herds, but was now abandoned other than the few times a year they snuck up there for a camp-out. The mostly non-existent trail, at this point, was only a quarter mile from Joey's ranch.

"Where you headed?" he asked.

"Don't know." Her knuckles were white on the reins, as though she expected him to wrangle them from her.

She brushed her hair from her face, shiny locks having slipped from her up-do and framing her cheeks. She looked so much like that lost kid he'd always known and protected he almost forget she was that stunning bride who'd awoken him less than an hour ago.

"The cabin's still an honest forty-minute ride." He slid off his horse. "If you're quick, you might get there before night falls."

Her horse looked tired, but the slightly wild and panicked look in Karlene's eyes faded with his suggested plan. She nodded, reaching across the horses for his star bag as he worked it free of the saddle, obviously not yet ready to face the music or the McNaughtons. Or even head back to her mostly-empty apartment in San Antonio which he'd helped her pack up and move to the ranch a few days ago. Even if they moved her stuff back, her lease expired in less than a week.

Lots to sort out and he'd bet she wanted to be alone, to let her thoughts settle into something that made sense again. Then when she had a plan, he'd help her execute it.

And right now, the cabin, the hills, the solitude—it would all help her recalibrate. He could almost see the stars hiding above them right now, and how they'd peek out one by one and then all in a rush. How the quietness of the hills would surround her like a comforting blanket. He'd bet she'd be right as rain within a day and ready to take action.

Why she'd bolted from the one thing she'd been dreaming about since her grandparents retired and sold their ranch when she was fourteen, he wasn't sure. He had ideas, but nothing concrete. The poor woman had thought she'd spend every summer on that Spragg ranch and then take it over when she was ready.

"Trade horses." He reached up for her hand and she took it.

In a fluid move, she leaned down toward him, trusting he'd catch her as she slid from Becky's back. He wrapped his arms around her; the dress curtaining them for a moment as the long skirt trailed behind. He gave her a brief hug, releasing her. She whacked the skirt into place and Joey handed her Cavalcade's reins to hold.

Her eyes welled as she took in his fresh, saddled horse, her head resting briefly along the horse's neck. He re-buckled the star pack to Cavalcade's saddle beside the bedroll. His star kit was like a bug-out bag for cowboys and she'd know what essentials to expect, as he always kept it stocked and ready for spending a night out in Hill Country.

The kit was a challenge, one he, Karlene and her brother Blake would take a few weekends a year. They'd grab the star bag and their bedrolls. They'd sleep under the stars, using his stocked items and nothing more, thumbing their noses at the modern world. If they had matches, a few cans of beans, a pocket knife, water, a first aid kit, flashlight and a few other essentials, they were equipped to deal with anything.

He wasn't sure if it was fully stocked for the needs of a runaway bride, however. Although there was a new addition —a filled flask. That would surely help.

"The radio's charged in case you run into trouble." He patted the secured star bag. "You know the channel I'll be on."

He eyed her dress and the formerly white satin shoes that

looked like they'd aged about twenty years in the past hour and tugged a bundle he'd wedged between the bag and saddle. "I brought you something to change into. Not sure how it'll fit, but better than a wedding gown."

* * *

"Well?" Joey asked as Karlene came out from behind her horse, dressed in his clothes.

His broad forehead creased, seeing her in a pair of his jeans, a flannel shirt and vest.

But there was still no heat in his gaze. He was acting reserved, careful, like she was a fragile kid in need. Not a grown woman he'd turned into a runaway bride with one heated look of longing.

She was such a fool for this man.

Karlene held her arms out at her side. "Better than the dress?"

The jeans were stretched to the limit across her hips, the shirt loose as the man was built, not an inch of him uncarved by hard work and long days of physical activity on the ranch. The shirt was a comforting blend of worn coziness and the familiarity of his aftershave. She had a feeling that in his haste, he'd gathered whatever was on his bedroom floor. Somehow that was more soothing than him thoughtfully selecting fresh items from his chest of drawers.

"It'll do," he said, his tone slightly gruff. He took his cowboy hat and dropped it on her head, knocking the last few pins from her hair and sending her locks cascading lopsidedly. The hat was warm, soft, and a bit too big.

She laughed despite it all and returned it to him. "You keep it. I'll destroy it." She knew what a pretty penny the

McNaughtons had paid for that hat. All the men in the wedding party had new felt hats as beautiful as this one.

He held her hand, balancing her as she stepped into a pair of his old boots. Smooth soles, indented with the impression of his toes. He then helped her into Cavalcade's saddle before launching himself onto the back of saddle-less Becky while clutching the wedding gown under his arm. He settled himself in the curve of the mare's back, reins in hand.

Karlene swallowed, taking in Joey's wide shoulders, the gentle roll of his biceps pushing against the tuxedo jacket's sleeves, the flatness of his stomach, the thickness of his quads. She loved everything about his appearance, from his slightly too long curly black hair to those pale blue eyes that felt like they were some kind of crazy gift from the universe. The man was a model cowboy, the kind of man she'd been determined to find in Thomas.

The kind of man she'd thought for one fleeting moment that she might have...

She cleared her throat. "Thanks, Joey."

"If anyone comes looking for you...?"

"Tell them you don't know," she said. She glanced at the dress. "You can burn that."

He rolled the gown into a lacy ball, jamming it under him like a stolen cushion from someone's great-grandmother.

When he looked up at her, it was with familiar concern for that tagalong kid she'd always been. But then his gaze turned into something softer, something unidentifiable that made her shift toward him without thinking until she slipped in the saddle, catching herself.

"Be safe," he said. "Stay on the trail. Don't get lost and get to the cabin before nightfall. It's going to be a cold night." He frowned up at the sky as though expecting snowflakes to fall.

"I won't get lost," she said darkly. "And I won't freeze. This is Texas."

He narrowed his eyes, both of them well aware of the crazy weather the state could throw at them at this time of the year.

"And if you need anything…"

She opened her mouth to finish his patent joke that she should call someone else, even though he was the only person she could always count on.

But he beat her to the punchline, changing it with a serious and somber, "You call me."

CHAPTER 2

Karlene angled Cavalcade higher into the hills, racing against the approaching night. Her heart lifted as the cabin's faint outline, surrounded by oaks at the crest of a hill, became visible. The fifty-year-old, open-windowed log cabin was one of her favorite spots.

As she slid off the horse a couple of snowflakes, tiny and cold, fell from the sky. Not enough to stick to anything, but enough to warn her not to waste time in building a fire.

The cabin had a fireplace and there was plenty of fallen dry wood beneath the oaks that she could collect with the flashlight from Joey's star bag. Often, when she and Joey came up here, they'd forego the cabin and sleep under the stars. They'd survive the weekend on whatever Joey had stocked in his aptly named under-the-stars bag which they now referred to as the star bag.

Tonight, though, she wanted that roof and four walls around her to reflect back whatever heat she could create in the cabin's fireplace.

When she and Joey slept outside, they'd stretch out beside

each other, the stars twinkling above as they'd talk about ranch life and the constellations, the weather and things they'd heard on the radio. No topic was off limits and she'd often forget the six-year age gap between them. Over the years, she'd never once considered coming here alone, but tonight she appreciated having the spot all to herself.

After ensuring Cavalcade was okay in his spot under the trees, Karlene grabbed the star bag and went about collecting wood in the enveloping night, her almost-wedding already feeling like a different lifetime.

As she dropped her first load of wood in the fireplace, a pair of squirrels zipped out from the chimney and past her boots, startling her.

"Oh, no." She slipped to her knees, sending the flashlight beam up the chimney. Wasn't it too late in the season for a nest? As she shone her light across the brick, she spotted something nestlike as the squirrel duo stood behind her, scolding loudly. She backed away from the fireplace, hands raised. "Sorry, sorry."

The parent squirrels moved in jittery leaps toward the hearth, their dark eyes on her. Then, quick as the night, they were back up the chimney and Karlene was without fire.

She sighed and laid out her bedroll in a corner, climbing halfway into her own little nest of bedding while digging for snacks in Joey's bag. Tomorrow would be better. Tomorrow all of this would be in the past.

She checked her watch, then turned off her flashlight, snuggling into the bedding. Right now she was supposed to be at the Sweetheart Creek Community Barn enjoying her wedding reception and filling up on succulent Wagyu beef.

She was supposed to be dancing with her new husband.

She was supposed to be changing out of her dress and heading to the city to stay in a hotel.

She was supposed to be getting on a plane at dawn for their whirlwind three-day, placeholder honeymoon, the real one to happen after calving and the Dragons hockey season had ended.

With tears in her eyes, Karlene rolled over, wondering if she was stupid to have run. She was hiding away, freezing her butt off like a big old chicken.

She shuddered, thinking how she hadn't even provided Thomas with the dignity of an explanation before she'd run away.

She pulled the blankets up further, contemplating how she was going to forgive herself for this one.

Karlene rolled over and felt around in the nearby star bag, digging out Joey's radio. She turned it on, its tiny green light casting a faint glow. She longed to press the Talk button, to hear a steady voice on the other end.

She wanted to talk to somebody who understood her, her dreams and fears, but most of all, wouldn't be angry with her. The man who'd given her permission to run away. The man who must see the bigger picture she was failing to grasp right now. The man who knew that somehow it was all going to be okay.

She turned the radio off again, knowing Joey wasn't the only one who used the open airways. People would be worried, angry and confused, and anything she said to Joey wouldn't be private.

After little sleep, she re-saddled up Cavalcade and rode through the predawn light and over the frosted land, back down out of the hills. With the blanket from her bedroll wrapped around her shoulders like a shawl, she let the horse pick the best route, and soon Joey's barn was a welcoming sight on the horizon.

As the horse picked his way through the yard, Joey emerged from the large red structure in a checkered shirt and jeans as though he'd been expecting her.

She felt like she was coming home.

* * *

Joey watched Karlene slide off his horse, his clothes curving around her body in a way that would distract any man. She led Cavalcade to the barn, and it took him a moment to catch up with the fact she'd returned from the cabin so early.

"You look cold," he stated.

She nodded. There were circles under her eyes, and he was certain it was more than just smeared mascara—a sign that yesterday's actions were weighing on her. He slowed his steps, hating that he was soon going to add to that weight.

"Get any sleep?"

She shrugged, her messy hair fluttering in the morning breeze.

Joey opened the barn door and wordlessly they went inside. He removed the saddle and placed the star bag in its spot, making a mental note to restock it, while Karlene brushed down Cavalcade. While he waited for her to be done, he did chores nearby, trying to get a read on how she was doing. He'd never seen her quite like this before, moving as though her body felt too heavy to bear.

Finally she turned, her dawdled and overly-perfected jobs completed.

"Hungry?" Joey asked.

"Yeah. A bit."

He headed back to the house, knowing she'd follow.

As she fell into step beside him, he changed directions and purpose. "There's the tiny house."

"I know my way around your yard, Joey," she said, her tone slightly unforgiving.

She'd always been able to read him well, and right now seemed to be sensing the bad news he had in store. Her shoulders were already pushing back, her face becoming a stony mask. This felt like those times when her brother Blake would make Joey pass on the message that Karlene wasn't welcome to tag along with them.

He veered toward the tiny home, directly across the driveway from his sprawling ranch house. It mimicked the style with a sharp peak above the front living area, giving the space a vaulted feeling. They were both a yellowish-orange log color and had big windows.

However, where Joey's home expanded out to the sides with five bedrooms, a massive kitchen and loft he'd made into his man cave, the tiny house went straight back. It was fifteen feet deep and thirteen feet wide, the entire living space compacted into three rooms. The living room and entry flowed into the galley kitchen, and at the rear was a bedroom and bathroom. One and done, as he liked to say.

"My hired hand moved out," he said, opening the door. "Got a modeling job in Cali."

"Did not." Karlene scoffed.

"That's the story he's sticking with." The ranch hand was decently handsome, but not what Joey figured a model should look like.

"He went to jail, didn't he?" she joked, her tone flat.

Joey chuckled, low and deep. "Let me show you what's what."

She narrowed her eyes, arms crossed, but cautiously followed him inside. She'd been here when the tiny home had first arrived on the truck. They'd even raided the local second-hand stores together to get it outfitted for staff to stay in. It had been surprisingly fun, Karlene finding it all a grand challenge of balancing cowboy practicality, homey warmth and necessary minimalism.

"Why are you talking like I'm going to be living in it?" she asked.

He flicked on lights, taking in the small space. The air was colder in here, the night's chill sticking to the unheated interior. Their shoulders pressed together as they stood in the entry.

"It's yours for as long as you need."

"You mean if I decide to be a chicken and hide away forever?" She stared at him through narrowed eyes, waiting for the penny to drop. "Because that's not my style as well as a pretty terrible plan."

Joey's gaze slipped from hers, and she was on him in a second. "What happened?" she demanded.

Joey scratched his chin with a thumb. "Your mom called looking for you. Guessed I'd know where you're at."

Karlene's eyelids drifted lower as she winced. "How bad was it?"

He walked further into the small home, cranking up the thermostat on his way by. He opened the fridge; the light illuminating the empty white cavern.

"I should go talk to her." Karlene sighed. "To everyone."

"I'd let them cool down a bit. Nothing good's going to be said today."

Karlene's expression dropped, and he hated the way he was hurting her, adding to the pain she was already carrying.

He'd argued with Mrs. Spragg to no end. But Kar's mom had insisted the family needed time, and it was best if her daughter stayed with him while they cooled down and wrapped their head around it all so they didn't hurt her feelings. Could she stay with him until they got over the shock? That had been last night.

"If I keep hiding, it's not going to make anything better." Karlene straightened her spine, that fiery look of determination he loved so much flitting across her face. "Can you give me a ride into town?"

Joey stood in the back bedroom's doorway, facing her.

"What?" she asked, concern in her expression.

"I'm sorry, Kar, but your mom said it would be best for you to stay here for a bit. She doesn't want to fight."

"How long?"

He shrugged.

"But tomorrow's Christmas!" Karlene dropped onto the edge of the nearby armchair, sliding off Joey's big boots, blinking back tears.

Joey, at a loss, focused on practicality.

"Bedding's clean." He flushed the stale water out of the toilet, then tipped a head toward the door. "Let's get you fed."

"I just took off my boots." She looked at the boots, coated with dust. "Your boots." She sagged off the armrest and into the deep cushions.

He turned his back to her at the door, jerking a thumb over his shoulder. "Come on."

Without hesitation, she came to life, leaping the few feet between them and launching herself onto his back. He gave her a piggyback ride across the driveway and into the big house. Her legs were wrapped around him, her body warm against his torso. If she had to be exiled, he was glad he was the one she'd come to.

* * *

Karlene knew she looked a fright in her slept-in borrowed clothes, and no doubt sleep and tear-smeared makeup and messy hair. But the way Joey was looking at her with his sweet, dancing eyes as well as how he was fighting a grin as he let her down off his back and opened his front door... Well, she wasn't sure how to feel.

Self-consciously, she wiped the skin under her eyes. "What are you laughing at?"

"Your hair looks worse than when you sleep out all night." The corner of his mouth crooked upward, his tone fond as he allowed her to go past him into the warm home.

She ran her fingers through her tangled locks, then stole the hat off his head. She pulled it down low over her own brow and marched off to the bathroom.

In front of the mirror, she removed the hat and flinched. Yesterday's mix of hairspray, teasing, straightening and curling to give her a fancy do had not traveled well. Today it looked more like a toddler had styled her hair. She borrowed Joey's brush, hacking at the knots as though they were solely responsible for her aching and confused heart.

Satisfied with the way she now appeared less like someone insane, she returned the hat to her head and went back to the kitchen, snagging a cup of coffee and a piece of toast from an abandoned plate by the sink.

Joey appeared from another room, pocketing his phone, his dog Brody at his heels. Joey eyed her half-eaten dry toast.

"Savage," he declared, pushing the butter dish her way. "Try it with butter."

She ignored him and finished the toast.

He opened the fridge, waving a carton of eggs. "Want some?"

She shook her head, her nerves chasing away her hunger. "What chores are up first? I need to earn my keep."

"You don't." His tone was soft, his gaze tender with something she didn't like or appreciate.

"Joe McCall doesn't do pity and right now…"

She blinked back the dampness in her eyes and marched to the front door, determined to stay moving so she could stay ahead of her thoughts and feelings about running away from marriage, and how Joey hadn't given her a single look of heat since. At the door she turned to see what Joey's hold up was. He was standing where she'd left him.

"Amber left you some clothes," he said gruffly, pointing toward his room.

He eyed her in his outfit and she could have sworn she saw a flicker of hunger in his gaze, a precious flit of possessiveness that made her entire being feel light as air.

"Amber Wylder?" She worked as an assistant in the town's boutique, Blue Tumbleweed. How did she know Karlene needed clothes?

She groaned internally. Everyone knew. It was a small town. As well, April had been in the church and had no doubt seen her run.

But did everyone know she was hiding out with Joey? She didn't even want to imagine what the rumors were saying about the two of them. Poor Thomas.

"She thought you might need something to wear."

Karlene blinked away the wetness in her eyes over the

woman's thoughtfulness. And a few minutes later, she reemerged from Joey's bedroom, properly outfitted in jeans, a sports bra and checkered shirt a lot like Joey's as well as a thick jacket.

"How do I look?" She gave a spin, delighted that April had pegged her size correctly.

"Like a cowgirl."

"That all you got, Joey McCall?"

"Yup." But there was a hint of humor flashing in his brown eyes as he swiftly took her in. If she didn't know better, she'd say he liked what he saw.

"Your dad called while you were brushing your hair earlier."

She sighed. So much for staying ahead of her thoughts and feelings.

Joey met her at the door, wiping a thumb under one of her eyes.

"What did he say?"

"He was just checking in." His thumb gently stroked her cheek as though following a smear of dust.

"Does he want me to come home?" she whispered, longing to lean into the heat of Joey's body, the solid security of him.

"He didn't say."

"Are they still mad at me?"

"Didn't say."

Her parents had been elated Karlene was getting married, and especially to ranch royalty like the McNaughtons. They'd been counting on signing the research agreement with the McNaughtons after the wedding and getting the massive grant that would have gone with it. Now both were gone. Plus, they had a house full of relatives and likely were facing a lot of gossip and judgment.

At least Karlene's phone was still in the church. She could only imagine the number of missed calls and texts that were piling up.

She inhaled deeply and spun, checking her surroundings for hints as to what was next. Anything but think about how her family was feeling about her and her actions right now.

And why hadn't Thomas come looking for her? Didn't he care? Or was he that mad at her?

She cleared her throat, stepping onto the front porch. "Where do you usually start with morning chores? The barn? Did you already finish in the barn?"

Joey shook his head and fell into step beside her, his dog trailing behind, its whip of a tail dancing through the air like a metronome.

Karlene waited while Joey opened a door on the side of the barn before walking inside, the familiar scent filling her. Animals. Old wood. Straw. Feed. History and a sense of belonging. She sighed, feeling her stress levels drop a notch. "I love a good barn."

She glanced over at Joey who was smiling a quiet smile, his eyes drifting over the open rafters, taking in the place alongside her. "There's something peaceful and wonderful about them, isn't there?" he said, his tone slightly wistful.

They let the horses out to pasture, then mucked out the stalls, falling into an easy rhythm she loved so much. Thomas was always in such a rush to get through chores, preferring to work in the ranch's big office. But Joey was like her, happy to take a moment and enjoy the tender sniff from a horse's velvety nose, or to pause and watch kittens race and tumble as they took each other down.

"Why couldn't I have found it in me to let go of him sooner?" she asked suddenly, turning to Joey, who was in the stall beside her.

He exited the enclosure with three long steps, his shovel balanced level as he eyed her, dumping the contents into the waiting wheelbarrow. He dropped the end of his shovel into the clean straw at their feet, leaning against the handle.

"He represents the dream you want."

She inhaled a shuddery breath and nodded.

It was true. She wanted the ranch life as well as working with the Dragons in San Antonio several days a week. She wanted to start a family, have pets, horses and other animals, her routines determined by the sun and weather and seasons. There was something calming about the solidity of it all.

"But?" Joey asked. "Something was missing?"

"Tom's a great guy."

Joey grunted.

She paused, angling her head at Joey. Was it weird that he and Tom had never become friends? Never gone for a beer?

She dropped onto a bound bale of straw, collapsing her face into her hands. "He'll never forgive me."

"Do you want him to?" Joey sat beside her, his shoulder almost touching.

"I didn't intend to hurt him. And I did. As well as humiliated him and his family."

"What's worse? That or marrying him and not meaning it?"

She sniffled.

"They wasted so much money on the wedding. On everything." She sniffed again, fearing she was going to outright bawl. Joey was steady and a wonderful friend, but he was her brother's best friend and a stoic cowboy. She considered him one of her closest friends, but she couldn't ugly cry on him.

She had to be tougher than that. Show him she was mature and had grown up. Except for the part where she'd run away from the most grown-up thing in her life: marriage.

"I hear everyone had a party last night," Joey said. "Ate the food, danced, drank the wine."

She nodded, gratified that it hadn't *all* gone to waste. But then the gates that had been holding back her tears released. Joey had her in his arms in less than a beat, pressing her body against his. He rocked her slowly, his large hand smoothing her wild hair.

"Let it out, Kar."

"Nobody's going to let me forget yesterday, are they?" From now on there'd be jokes at her expense, awkward pauses in conversations, possibly even the McNaughtons crossing the street or giving her fake smiles and excuses whenever they bumped into each other.

"Depends if you stay in Sweetheart Creek." Joey winked and her heart crashed with the truth of what she'd done and her tears returned. He wrapped her in his arms again, his cheek against the top of her head. "But so what, Kar? So what?"

"I want to live out here," she muttered. "Not in the city."

He held her out, studying her with such seriousness she laughed. "You afraid of some gossip?"

"Yes! And I don't know the rules. Do I still have to break up with Thomas? Or is that implied? And where am I supposed to live now? How am I going to get my stuff back from Thomas's? It's going to be so awful." Her head returned to Joey's chest.

And what would it take to get this man holding her to see her as more than a lost kid?

"You can stay in the tiny house as long as you want."

She perked up with the idea of rarely having to go into town or see anyone else. And the little home was small, simple, and without clutter. Did she actually need her old belongings? Living with nothing in the tiny house would be like a stripping down to find out what she truly needed and wanted in her life.

Did she still want to work for the Dragons?

Maybe.

Did she still want the ranching lifestyle?

She inhaled the barn's scents, the calm quiet. Heck yeah. She'd always want this. It was in her blood, in her bones. Even more than working with the Dragons, which was a job she absolutely loved.

They stood, ready to get back to chores.

"Can I stay here for Christmas?" She swallowed, thinking of her family's rejection, her broken plans. The scheduled honeymoon. The family Christmas filled with wedding guests who were staying at the ranch for the holiday, making it also a family reunion.

"Kar, you can stay with me until the end of time."

The seriousness of his words and the heartfelt way in which he delivered them gave her a lift she didn't think possible.

CHAPTER 3

arlene's head was spinning. She'd been caught out, coming out of the barn, laughing with Joey, heading to the house to make a full cowboy breakfast of sausage, bacon, eggs and hash browns which would tide them through the approaching Christmas Eve afternoon and until supper.

Her parents had been standing in the middle of the driveway, and when they'd spotted her laughing like she had no problems in the world, had launched straight into a very thorough what-for. How could she have strung along Thomas like that? Mrs. McNaughton was beside herself. Not to mention the expense the McNaughtons had gone to, or the family members who had come all the way to Sweetheart Creek for the wedding. Didn't she owe it to Thomas to straighten it all out and walk down that aisle?

No.

Their entire grant for the next several years was dependent on collaborating with the McNaughtons. What were they supposed to say to them now that she'd run out, cost them an arm and a leg on a wedding, and humiliated their son?

I'm sorry.

They'd raised her better than this.

I know.

They'd been desperate for her to fix it all and Karlene had ended up making herself dizzy, she'd shook her head so long and hard during the conversation, trying to shake off the humiliation she'd caused herself and everyone she cared about. Then she'd fled into the big house to the soundtrack of the low scolding tone of Joey telling her parents to understand how much courage their daughter had shown by following her gut.

Not long after, Joey crouched down to where she'd sat on the floor, back against the kitchen cupboards. He sat beside her, talking to her like he was trying to coax a stray out from under his couch.

He held her as the sobs rocked through her, his body warm and strong, giving her the strength she didn't possess.

"I'm so stupid." She leaned back, and he tenderly used the hem of his shirt to dry her eyes.

"No, you're not."

"Yes, I am."

She'd been waiting and hoping for Joey to return her feelings that she'd become blind to what she was truly doing in her own life. Preparing to walk down the aisle with Thomas? What had she been thinking? That relationship had been wrong for so long and she hadn't even noticed until she'd been standing in that church with eyes only for her best friend.

She was so angry with herself.

"What you did was brave."

"Why did you nod at me in the church?"

Joey paused, silent.

Anger swirled through her, the desire to rage against him building. She could blame him, even though the fault wasn't his.

Who was she kidding? His nod had probably just been nothing more than a supportive you've-got-this from a man who still thought of her as a lost kid.

But she'd felt the entire world in that small gesture. Hopes. Dreams. Possibilities.

Permission.

And it was like that nod had been saying something more. Way more.

Run.

Run, Karlene. I'll be here for you with open arms and an open heart.

* * *

Joey needed to be out on a horse, and he felt Karlene did, too. It had been tough not telling her why he'd nodded to her in the church. The surprising feelings that had welled up inside him at seeing her as a bride.

He loved her.

He knew it for sure, the feelings swirling and brewing, growing stronger over the past twenty-four hours. Now that he had taken off the blinders, it was so obvious to him.

And probably her parents, too, judging from the way they'd laid into her. He could see how it looked—her running straight from the church and into his welcoming arms like it had all been planned.

Optics aside, this wasn't the time to make Karlene his.

His everything.

She was on the rebound, reeling from her broken promise to marry another. She needed time. Time to make sure she was doing the right thing. Not the convenient thing she might think she wanted right now while she was in the thick of it all.

"What's going on?" Karlene asked, entering the barn. She'd been cleaning up the kitchen while he saddled their horses and strapped the bedrolls and packs to their backs.

Now she stood with her hands on her hips in her new clothes, watching him bring her horse around. It was a nice outfit, very cowgirl. But it wasn't the same as seeing her in his shirt and jeans. He'd never get over the burn of possessiveness he'd felt dig its way into his soul earlier. That insistent longing, like a persistent stowaway, pushing against his willpower.

But one look at her and he knew this was the wrong time to let himself off-leash. She was exhausted from the guilt and the emotional battle with her parents, as well as the tears. Crying always wiped her out, and right now she probably wanted to curl up under a heavy, thick blanket, eat candy and laugh at a goofy movie. He could give that to her, but it would kill him to watch her wallow. He needed to give her something healing to bring the bounce back into her step and the smiles and warmth in her every look.

"You need some hill therapy." He handed her the reins to her horse, Becky, as well as a warm pair of gloves.

"I do?" The lift in her torso as she straightened, delighted by his idea, was all he needed to know.

She lifted herself into the saddle and followed Joey and Cavalcade out of the yard, Brody following them with a happy bark.

They had several hours before sunset. Plenty of time to

reach their destination—not the cabin. They'd let the squirrels enjoy a quiet Christmas without them there.

"Tomorrow's Christmas," she pointed out. "And we're camping out?"

"That work for you?"

She was silent for a moment, as though considering whether it did or not. "Did you bring cranberries?" she asked. "Turkey? Potatoes?"

"Of course. All canned." He patted the bag strapped to the rear of his saddle.

She remained silent for a beat. "Is there such thing as canned turkey?"

"Guess you'll find out." He flashed a smile and led them through a narrow trail in the brush, then rode alongside the creek. They continued up the hills, riding side by side and through a meadow and toward a thicket. They'd camped out here with Blake when Karlene was fifteen. It had been their first of many camp-outs, but they hadn't been here since, and he figured it was due time to return.

They set up camp, along with a tent.

"You can sleep in there," Joey said, tossing her roll inside.

"No." She dragged it out again.

"It's going to be cold again tonight."

"So you get to stay out here under the stars, and because I'm a woman I have to sleep in the tent?"

"You were half frozen when you rode in this morning." He shook his head once at her stubbornness, grateful she had the spunk to push back, but worrying she was going to freeze herself out of pride. Maybe they should have stayed home. But her in the tiny house and him in the big house—somehow, it didn't feel right to have that distance between them when she was feeling so down.

Or maybe he was just greedy and wanted as much of her as possible. Because maybe deep down he still feared she'd leave his ranch and marry Thomas after all, and that would be that. Their friendship would wither and die and he'd be stuck loving a woman who was someone else's wife.

Either way, he wanted every moment with her, even if she kept him up half the night with her snoring on the hard ground.

She plunked down in front of the fire he was building, rooting through the food pack.

"I was only cold because squirrels had nested in the cabin's chimney."

"You chose indoors?" he asked, still trying to sort out what her night in the cabin had been like. She'd been strangely silent about it all. Her brother Blake was a sleep-inside kind of guy, but his sister was all about being under the stars. "Why?"

"It was snowing."

"Snowing?" He looked up at the sky. He'd checked the forecast, but now he worried he'd set them up for a night that was going to be more than they wanted to handle.

"Teeny flakes." She laughed. "I'm getting soft in my old age."

She pulled rations from their pack. A can of cranberries, canned turkey, and canned potatoes. Then butter and a loaf of bread. His plan was to make bush pies by squeezing the sandwich between the two cast-iron plates in his bush pie maker and then cooking it over the fire.

Joey let his shoulder and thigh rest against Karlene's as they sat cross-legged on the ground. "Suit yourself then. Prove your toughness and stay out here and freeze. I'll take the tent."

"Or we could both share the tent."

Her words hung like an invitation. Just within reach. All he had to do was say "Okay."

He turned to her, his face close to hers, his voice gentle. "You snore."

"Ha! *You* do." She reached across herself to poke him in the ribs. He jolted, but didn't move or retaliate.

His eyes met hers, but she quickly looked away, her focus back on the fire.

"Thanks for the thing with my parents," she mumbled.

"Yeah." He'd been angry at the way they'd lit into her and let their own problems be bigger than their need to parent their hurting daughter.

Didn't anyone else get it? If you loved someone, you backed them because they were important to you. It didn't matter what had happened and if you thought they should have done better. Karlene had already managed to do the best she could do in that moment. And as a result she'd done something incredibly brave. You didn't run away from your own wedding for no reason.

They cooked their turkey bush pies, and Karlene was several bites into hers when she asked, "Why do you think Tom hasn't come to see me?"

He could hear the lump in her throat, the unspoken fear that Thomas didn't think she was worthy of fighting for.

"Maybe he's giving you space?" Joey offered.

But he knew that if you truly loved a woman, you'd go to the end of the earth to find her, to talk, to find a way to make it right.

In his books, it was clear that Thomas McNaughton didn't love Karlene Spragg anywhere near as much as he should.

* * *

Maybe Thomas *had* come by the ranch to see her and Joey had told him where to go, acting like a beautiful wall between her hurting heart and confused mind.

Karlene shook her head. Joey wouldn't do that. He'd run gentle interference and protect her, but not stand between her and her fiancé. Even if Joey seemed to secretly believe Thomas was a pretty-boy cowboy. She'd heard him mutter that in his barn once after Thomas had stopped by to pick her up in an expensive pair of cowboy boots and a new Stetson— his ranch manager clothes, as Karlene thought of them. Thomas spent more time between four walls than out branding, herding and mucking out barns, and she'd once teased him that he wasn't a real cowboy at all. He'd agreed, stating proudly that he was a rancher.

Joey's brows lowered as he took a massive bite of his sandwich, cranberry oozing out the backside of it and dropping onto his tin plate.

She set her sandwich to the side and Brody claimed it, finishing it in one big, greedy gulp. "Brody!"

"He's going to be gassy now," Joey complained. "He's sleeping in the tent with you."

"He can have it. I'll be out here."

"Freezing your butt off."

"Possibly." He hadn't bitten on her offer to share the tent. What was up with him? Was it the age gap? The fact that Blake would freak out if they got together?

She could easily see her life with Joey. Campouts, chores, laughter. Very different from Thomas's approach to ranch life. He carried a lot of expectations, which kept him on a tightrope. Whereas Joey had the freedom of letting only himself down, not a massive family legacy.

A burble of laughter escaped her.

"What?"

"I was trying to imagine you working in an office."

"I have an office."

"And how much time do you spend in it, Mr. McCall?"

Joey gave a slow, crooked grin that made her heart hiccup. "As little as humanly possible."

"That's what I figured, cowboy."

They tidied up their first course, then set about using the cast iron press for dessert pies. Karlene buttered the bread while Joey opened a can of cherry pie filling and broke up a chunk of dark chocolate. She fit one slice of bread into the mold while Joey piled on the filling and bits of chocolate. Then another slice of bread on top and they closed up the contraption, putting it in the fire to brown as well as melt the chocolate.

"Why'd you stay so long?" Joey asked. "Because of his ranch?"

Karlene sat silently for a moment, considering. She wasn't sure if she had a short answer that went beyond being sucked in by the dream of living on a ranch.

"Sorry," Joey said, his tone gruff. "It's not my business."

"You're my friend, harboring me in my time of exile. It's very much your business." She pointed to the sky, which had darkened, a shooting star soaring across it. "Make a wish."

"Already did," he said, not looking up from his cooking.

"What does a cowboy wish for?"

"Little cowboys and cowgirls to help with the work."

"Not an adult cowgirl first?"

"It's in the bag."

She laughed, heat rising in her cheeks at his surety. "An implied given if you get the little ones?"

She watched him, softened by his admission of wanting a

family. Of course he did. It wasn't as though she'd ever thought him immune or to stay a bachelor forever. She supposed she simply hadn't tried to see his dreams from his viewpoint. Instead, always seeing his future from her own, and wondering where she might or might not fit into things.

The idea of him finding a wife that wasn't her was unsettling. What if the woman didn't want her and Joey to be friends any longer? What if she made little digs like Thomas often had, a hint of jealousy that tainted their happiness? And what if Joey's wife saw that Karlene's feelings ran much deeper than friendship?

"How old is your dream cowgirl?" she asked, trying to sound casual.

"Age doesn't matter."

"Oh, I don't believe that for a minute."

"It's true."

"Is not! For all the times you've ridden me about being so young, you're now claiming that age is unimportant?"

"You're not a kid anymore, Karlene." The way he looked at her, the firelight dancing in his eyes and his voice dropping to an intimate octave, she could have sworn she'd caught a glimpse of hunger. She blinked and looked away.

What if *she* had been his shooting star wish?

And what if his wish came true?

CHAPTER 4

"You didn't put up a tree?" Karlene had showered their camp-out off of her and was standing in Joey's living room on Christmas Day. The vaulted ceiling stretched high above, and the triangular windows at the top were streaked with sunshine.

"I did."

"Where? It doesn't feel like Christmas in here at all!" She turned in the room again, on the lookout for evidence that today was, in fact, Christmas. Out in the hills, it could be anytime. But in here, it should *feel* like the holiday was *here*.

"I already celebrated with my parents before they went on their Christmas cruise. So it feels like the holiday's come and gone. However…"

He hooked a finger through hers, gently pulling her along through the narrow hallway covered in watercolors painted by his mom. He pushed open the main bedroom door, the one he'd taken over from his parents when they'd retired to Florida, and there was the cutest tree, sitting on his dresser. It was only about three feet tall and the lights were plugged in, the ornaments shining as they waved in the room's air currents.

"I do have my tree."

"Why in here?" she asked, coming closer. The ornaments were all different. Some from cities, some from theme parks. It was like one giant memento—or scrapbook.

"Because."

"Because why?"

He shrugged his broad shoulders in his vest. "I like it."

"Are these all…are they special?" She was facing the tree again, touching ornaments, turning them for a better view.

"I got this one in the Atlanta airport when we went to Canada that Christmas." He touched an airplane, then a snowman. "This is Bonhomme de Neige."

"Who?"

"A snowman in Quebec."

"Oh." She saw a reindeer near the back of the tree. "What about this one?"

"I just liked it."

"And this?" It was an old photo of a ranch from probably the 1940s, locked between two plates of glass and ringed with soldering lead to hold it together. It was ugly, but somehow still pulled at the romanticism inside her. The photo and style were so quintessentially a ranch it made her eyes moist with unshed tears for her own dream.

Joey tapped it further into the branches. "Just something from a flea market. I don't know why I bought it."

"It spoke to you?"

"That sounds corny."

"I know."

"It did though."

She could feel his breath on her cheek as he took in his tree.

"You always knew this would be your ranch," she whispered, thinking how secure he must have felt as a teen knowing where he'd end up. Here. The place that was his heart and soul. The land his parents and grandparents had lived on.

"Oh my gosh! Did I give you this one?" She lifted the pewter snowflake off the tree, studying the school photo inside. She laughed and groaned at her grade six image. "Braces. Ugh." She rehung it on the tree, hiding it near the back.

Joey's hand reached around, snagging it, placing it in the front.

"Can I update the photo at least?"

"Never."

She'd saved up for months for that gift, wanting to get Joey something special. Why she'd ever decided to put her face on an ornament and give it to an eighteen-year-old she didn't know.

"It's what started the tree."

"I had such a crush on you."

"I know."

"Is that why you were so nice to me?" Why he'd let her tag along, join in when she only slowed them down.

"You were a fun kid."

"Yeah, whatever happened to her? She got the braces off and grew up and got boring."

"You don't see yourself, do you?" His hand gently rested on her shoulder, sliding down her arm, and she leaned against him. His hand snaked around her middle, then the other, holding her like she belonged in his arms and always had. "Nothing boring about Karlene Abigail Spragg."

She tipped her head back, resting it against his shoulder. "Yeah? How's that?"

"Not only can she outrun the town while riding bareback in high heels, but she gets paid to beat up on poor, defenceless NHL players."

She laughed. "They're far from defenceless."

"You do things your own way. Always have." There was a hint of admiration in his tone, heady and addicting.

"You make me sound stronger than I feel."

She leaned against Joey, listening to the steady beat of his heart. She hadn't done love or her wedding her own way. She'd started dating Thomas in high school because he was cute. They'd stayed together because it was easy and fun and everyone said how great they were together. There was nothing bad or wrong about their relationship. It just probably hadn't meant to go beyond high school. And then her family had started talking about marriage and how if they collaborated, they could change the face of ranching and some such almighty, lofty things.

Really, there had been no turning back. Not when she didn't have a reason beyond the fact that there was no big spark between herself and Tom, and that they were probably meant to be friends and not more.

The only thing she'd actually chosen in recent memory was her job as a physical therapist and her city apartment. Well, no. Thomas had selected her apartment from her narrowed down list because it was closer to the highway that ran out toward Sweetheart Creek. But her job she'd chosen, knowing she wanted to work with her hands, help people who felt like their dreams were being taken away from them due to an injury. Sort of like how she'd felt when her grandparents had sold their ranch, a place she'd always assumed she'd inherit or buy from them.

"Why athletes? Why not work on cowboys in town?" Joey asked, his voice low in her ear. "Lots of broken men around here to keep you busy."

"Broken by animals and tough living." She'd much rather heal hockey players.

"Broken is broken, is it not?"

"Not always."

"How so?"

"I know it makes no sense." She'd gone blue in the face trying to explain it to her family. Why want a ranch here but drive all the way to the city to work on athletes? "The attitude is different. Cowboys are all rub some dirt in it. I feel more like I'm part of the team and the healing process with a hockey player. They're more likely to stick with the program."

"That makes sense."

She laughed. "No, it doesn't."

"Maybe not," he insisted. "But I get it."

"Well, you're probably the first." She shifted so she could see him better, fearing that he was going to unlock his embrace and let her go.

But instead of releasing her, he tightened his arms, his lips drifting downward until they were on hers.

This was the moment she'd waited for almost all of her life. Their first kiss.

His arms felt so right around her, and she was protected and safe in his embrace, his lips dancing over her own in a way that made her sigh with happiness. His kiss was perfect. Firm, yet giving, teasing and testing, and for a beat or two she forgot to breathe at the perfectness of it all.

This moment, locked in Joey's arms, was the best Christmas gift of all.

* * *

Karlene, still giddy from their kiss, whisked the eggs, sugar, vanilla and milk together in Joey's kitchen. "Okay, add the cinnamon."

Joey carefully sprinkled in the teaspoon of spice and she mixed it in. She handed him the bowl. "Now poor it over the bread and raisins."

"It can't be this easy." He stared at the filled casserole dish a moment before putting it in the oven.

"Bread pudding isn't difficult."

"I could sit and eat this whole thing when it's done."

"Just another reason why my brother chose you as his best friend."

"Another reason, huh?" Joey was standing close, a part of him always brushing against her, but she sensed a tensing in his shoulders.

"Yes, and you're the bestest friend anyone could ever ask for." She took a step toward him, leaning forward, leaving herself open for a kiss.

He gave a curt nod, sliding to the right as though he'd been in her way.

"Joey?" She squeezed between him and the counter.

"Yeah?" He stepped back, but she grabbed his shirt, pulling him close.

"I'm very lucky he found you." She leaned in, giving him a quick kiss that relaxed his shoulders. He returned her kiss with a firmness that had her wrapping her arms around him and wishing he'd let go and lift her onto the counter and kiss her with whatever they had pent up between them.

He broke the kiss, whispering, "I should check on the chicken."

Joey had a chicken on the grill's rotisserie, part of their Christmas dinner.

Trying not to act disappointed that Joey didn't want to assault her mouth with more kisses, she handed him the foil wrapped pack of buttered and spiced potatoes. "You want to add the potatoes?"

He took them to the grill while Karlene wiped down the counter, studiously fighting her urge to go jump into Joey's arms and kiss him until New Year's Day. She admired that he was taking it slow when she wanted to do nothing more than hit the accelerator, but a part of her feared that he was holding back out of secret doubts. And there were likely a few such as the age gap and her being his best friend's sister. There was also the small fact that she was supposed to be on her honeymoon with someone else...

Karlene shook out her hands, trying to cool her thoughts as she checked the clock. Her extended family would soon be gathering around the dining room table to celebrate Christmas.

She sucked in a breath and looked for a chore to take care of and turned abruptly, almost bumping into Joey.

"Try this." He'd come inside, unnoticed, and had a fork extended to her.

She opened her mouth, and he gave her a morsel of chicken. Her eyes widened as she chewed. "So good!"

"Right?" He smiled with pride and tossed the fork in the dishwasher. He began running hot water for the pots they'd dirtied and she grabbed the tea towel, falling into the cleanup routine, glad for something to do.

The radio played in the background, a mix of country and western Christmas songs keeping them company.

"Either or," she said, announcing an old game they'd play out under the stars as teenagers. "Bread pudding or Christmas cake."

Joey's face scrunched in disgust. "Bread pudding all the way. Turkey or ham?"

"Turkey. Gravy or cranberries?"

"On the turkey?"

"Yes."

She opened the package of chocolate-covered raisins he always seemed to keep in the cupboard by his fridge. She popped a few into her mouth.

Joey was still considering his answer, and he leaned her way, mouth open. She dropped a few treats into his mouth as well. "Gravy," he said, crunching on the chocolate. "No. Cranberries. No, gravy."

"You have to choose!" She leaned against the counter beside him at the sink and he flicked soap bubbles at her. She laughed, wondering if this was what it felt like when you found the right person. Every day was a holiday, even if you were doing your own quiet thing. It was like hanging out with a best friend in your favorite place on earth.

"I can't choose."

"You have to!" She scooped a handful of soap bubbles and smeared it across his chin. "Santa!"

"Come sit on my lap," he growled, his wet hands leaving the sink, reaching for her.

She squealed and ducked around the kitchen island. With a grin, he went back to washing. She edged closer, unsure if the implied truce would be honored, or even if that was what she wanted.

Joey flinched as though he was about to move and she jumped away.

"Ha!" she crowed. "You can't get me!"

"Wanna bet?"

She squealed again, giggling as they tore through the house. This was more like it!

She lunged out the front door and down the steps in her stocking feet as his wet fingers touched her. She came to an abrupt halt in the driveway, Joey piling into her, hands going to her waist. When he saw they had company, he dropped his hands and stepped back, one hand going to his hair.

Casually, he said, "Hey, man. Merry Christmas."

* * *

Well, this was awkward. His best friend was glaring at Joey liked he'd murdered someone. All he'd done was lay his hands on the guy's sister's very shapely waist. Well, that was all Blake knew, anyway.

"What's going on?" Blake stared at Joey, then Karlene, his brows more bent out of shape than the time the two of them had found her swinging from the top of her grandparent's barn's loft on a frayed old rope. It was that same you'll-get-yourself-killed look.

Except now it was because his sister was with him. Or at least it sure looked like she was.

What was Joey doing? He knew better. Kar hadn't resolved things with Thomas and here he was, in there already, without even allowing her time to breathe.

Sure, Thomas wasn't the man Joey would have chosen for

54

her—but, as it turned out, he was a little biased about who should be Karlene's boyfriend—but he wasn't a bad person. Joey should be giving her the room to decide what and who she truly wanted, not taking advantage of her vulnerability.

And that's exactly what Blake saw. A guy taking advantage of his sister. Moving in while she was feeling hurt and confused.

Even if she seemed mostly okay despite running off without marrying her fiancé forty-eight hours ago.

Joey cleared his throat, cutting a quick look at Karlene.

"You want to know what's going on?" she asked her brother, crossing her arms. "We're goofing around, Blake."

Yup. There wasn't a speck of vulnerability in the sharp jut of her chin and wide, angry stance.

Blake's brows worked their way lower.

"Nothing is going on," Joey added, his tone level, hoping for Karlene's sake that this didn't turn into a giant fight. She'd been let down enough by her family already, and it was Christmas. Everyone should cool it, let it go and move on. "You know we're just friends."

Karlene sucked in a sharp breath, and Joey mentally kicked himself. Now she'd be doubting herself. But maybe they did need a little space—the kind of space that the reminder of friendship might bring. He'd been trying to take it slow today, but one taste of her lips and he was addicted, all thoughts of giving her time to ease into something all but obliterated.

Blake opened his mouth, hesitated, then said to Karlene, "I came to see if you wanted to talk to Thomas. Maybe patch things up before dinner?" His gaze darted to Joey, as though expecting him to jump in and interfere.

Joey took a step back so he wouldn't give into temptation or that possessive roaring fire inside him and do just that—

interfere and lose Karlene. She needed the freedom to choose, and she needed the space to do so. Even if it was the last thing he wanted to give her.

Karlene jerked the hem of her shirt into place. "I'm not—we're not."

"You're still engaged."

Karlene twisted the ring on her finger, removing it, her voice wobbling. "Then I need to give this back to him."

Her brother took a step away from her, hands raised. "You do that yourself. I just came because I thought…"

"Where is he? Does he want to talk?"

The vulnerability in her voice gutted Joey.

Blake gave a slight shake of his head. "I don't know."

"Then why are you here?" Karlene's anger was back.

"Because it's not right."

"What isn't?"

"All of it." He cut a glare at Joey. "You've run away! There's tons of family at home and it's Christmas and it's all a big mess and everyone's upset. You need to come home and fix this."

Joey shuffled a few steps to the porch, anything to ease off the urge to jump in and set his friend straight. This wasn't about *them*.

Karlene jammed her hands on her hips, glaring at her brother. "So you're not here because you care. Because you realized that what Tom and I have is more a friendship than true love and that I just saved us both years of quiet agony and pretending?"

Joey worked to bite back a smile. There were so many things to love about his beautiful Karlene Spragg.

"That's really sweet, Blake," she continued. "And especially sweet that you're worried that I might be hurt or humiliated.

And that you're worried that I feel rejected instead of supported by our family, and that nobody cares to understand why I left that church."

Joey's smile had faded, and his heart ached for Karlene.

"Maybe it hurts that Tom never came to see how I am. To fight for me. So why are you here to fight for him when he's not? And you know what? Maybe that's the proof that everyone needs in order to understand that I did the very best thing for both of us by running out of that church."

Her brother inhaled slowly while Joey exhaled. Then Blake got back in his truck muttering "Okay, okay, okay. Merry Christmas little sis."

CHAPTER 5

*K*arlene thanked Joey as he swung by her parents' place on Friday night. As they came up the street she could see her car sitting under the streetlight at the end of the short driveway, thankfully not decorated with "Just Married" signs, paint, and streamers. Thomas was the one who'd had to face that on his Dodge Ram dually last Tuesday.

She cursed under her breath, realizing that while she might have a hidden key for her car, she needed her purse and phone, which were probably in the house. Or possibly even still at the church. Either way, she was going to have to face her parents and all the relatives still staying with them.

Even though tomorrow was Saturday, she was needed at the rink as several of her players were in physical rehab and were due for some beating up. That meant she had to get back to her apartment in the city. After that, she could figure out the rest of her week, her month, her life.

Her life. What was she going to do?

Live in Joey's tiny house forever? And what about Joey?

He'd been holding back with her since Blake's visit, and last night's Christmas dinner had been quiet, their earlier fun deflated. Today had been mostly chores, no kisses and she didn't know how to fix whatever was bothering Joey.

"I have a trip to Jamaica in June," she stated dryly to Joey, thinking of the honeymoon trip she and Thomas were to take. "Want to run away with me?"

"I don't think that would be a good idea," he replied gently.

"A trip for two," she sang. "Paid for."

Joey's grip on the steering wheel tightened, and he kept his gaze out the windshield. "I don't think that would be the sensitive thing to do—to take that trip with you."

Karlene leaned back in the seat and whispered, "I was joking." She turned to Joey as he stoped the truck in front of her parents' house. "What happened? Between us? We were having fun, weren't we?"

His eyes cut to hers, a certain sadness expanding in them. "Karlene, you're on the rebound." His gaze dropped to her bare left hand. "Possibly even still engaged."

She reached for the door, eyes wet, but he grabbed her hand, holding her back. She waited for him to speak.

"I want something real," he said, his voice low. "Someone who's in the free and clear to love me fully. No regrets. No what-ifs. Nothing hanging over her heart."

She sniffed and let herself out of the truck, his hand slipping from hers.

"Don't you want that, too?" he asked, his voice filled with uncharacteristic hesitance before becoming firm. "Don't choose me because I'm an easy defence against what you don't want to face."

A flare of anger and frustration blew through her. "What's that supposed to mean?"

"Kar…"

"No. No!" She smacked the side of the truck. "You don't get to say that kind of crap to me." She climbed back into the truck even though he'd put it back into gear. "I have loved you since I was a kid. Since I was a *kid*, Joey! You are not some easy shield I'm using to protect myself from the truth—the fact that I didn't pay enough attention and screwed things up with Thomas." She jumped out again, slamming the door, wishing she'd given him a searing kiss to seal her words and how she truly felt into his stupid, useless sense of honor-loving cowboy brain.

* * *

Karlene sat on a cold bleacher overlooking the ice rink while the Dragons performed their early morning practice before their afternoon home game. She sipped her cup of coffee despite it having gone cold over half an hour ago.

She watched the players, her mind replaying the awkward hug between her and her parents when she'd left their place, keys, purse and phone in hand, just minutes after arriving. The hug was something at least, something that made her eyes well whenever she thought about it. They were hurt, confused and embarrassed, but trying to see her side of it all.

"How's Landon looking?" Miranda Fairchild asked, sliding into the seat beside her. The team's owner hunched her shoulders, burrowing deeper into her wool coat.

"Hm?" Karlene sniffed back her emotions and her gaze drifted automatically to the goalie she'd rehabbed earlier in the year. "Oh, his ankle is strong."

"How about Dylan?"

"Solid." The center had broken his foot during training

camp, another rehab case. "I expect him back on the ice for games within a month, month and a half, tops."

"Good. I hate having these guys sitting on the bench the whole season. Thank goodness they're insured, or I'd be broke." Miranda smiled, looking more refreshed than Karlene might have predicted, given that the players and most of their support team had enjoyed only three days off over Christmas. Miranda, as a female sports team owner, had been getting a lot of attention in the press, not all of it good, and some days she looked simply worn out by it all.

Miranda brushed a lock of hair off her high cheekbone and Karlene gasped before her heart plummeted.

Miranda turned to her in question.

"You're engaged?" Karlene whispered.

She hadn't even heard the woman was dating. Then again, Karlene had been a bit busy with her own engagement leading up to last Tuesday when she'd spontaneously shredded it all.

"Dak." Miranda's entire being lit up in a way that awed Karlene.

She'd never felt that instant light-up feeling with Thomas. Not like that.

Shouldn't she have? Or was it because their love had been so gradual, so expected in its progression toward marriage that there hadn't been that element of he-chose-me-he-really-chose-me-and-loves-me! excitement some women got to feel.

"Who's Dak?" The name wasn't ringing any bells.

Miranda laughed, leaning her shoulder against Karlene's. Then she stood, embracing a tall, dark man who'd joined them. "This is Dak Morisette. Dak, this is Karlene Spragg. I mean, McNaughton." Miranda tipped her head to the side. "Did you change your last name?"

Karlene shook her head. "Still Spragg." She shook Dak's

hand, trying to maintain a smile, hoping Miranda assumed that her remaining maiden name was about her being progressive and not the hook into a story she wanted to hear more about.

"Karlene's the magic behind my healing injured players."

"Pleased to meet you," Dak said with a kind smile.

Then the two were whisked away by staff, wrapped in their own cloud of happiness, where they barely seemed to see anything beyond each other.

As it should be.

And how Karlene felt when she was with Joey.

Joey, who seemed to think she was using him.

Joey, who had kissed her.

Joey, who'd acted almost as though he was truly and deeply in love with her...

* * *

Karlene stood in her almost-empty apartment a few blocks from the rink and sighed.

"Now what?" she muttered, dropping a pair of sneakers into a cardboard box and wondering where she was going to live next. Her landlord expected her out on Monday at noon as promised, her apartment already leased to someone new. She had less than forty-eight hours to sort herself out.

Maybe Joey, even though things were messy with him, would stay true to his cowboy word and his tiny home was hers for as long as she needed.

Knowing she couldn't stay here, she began chucking the final few items into boxes, not caring if she'd need it in the morning or before bed. She taped the containers shut and stacked them at the door. If she was smart about it, she could cram it all into her car for one trip back to Sweetheart Creek.

Or she could try to find a last-minute place here in the city.

Right.

Sweetheart Creek it was.

To beg and borrow from her brother's best friend as the tagalong kid one more time...

She opened her door and squawked, nearly dropping the box in her arms. The man who'd been about to knock helped steady her load.

"Tom!" she gasped. "What are you...? Are you...? Come in!" She backed into the apartment, placing the box back into the stack it had come from.

"You moving in with someone?" His tone, she knew, had been meant to be joking, but obviously he'd heard something about where she'd been hiding out and had jumped to conclusions. A conclusion she was embarrassed to admit was likely somewhat accurate, even if unflattering.

"Sorry, I don't have anywhere to sit." She gestured to the empty rooms.

"Your stuff can stay at my place as long as you need. Use your key when you come get it all."

She nodded, mute. This was truly it. Over. Done.

It was a strange brew of relief and hurt that he wasn't fighting for her.

Karlene walked to her large leather purse, sitting on a stack of plastic bins near the door. She rummaged through it until she found the velvet ring box. She handed it to Thomas.

"I'm sorry," she whispered.

"I'm not," he replied, his voice cracking with strain.

"No. Really. I am. I'm so sorry. I didn't mean to hurt you or snub your family or—" She inhaled a deep breath. "I should have figured things out sooner and been honest with myself and with you."

"Karlene. There were two of us in that relationship."

"I know, and I'm so sorry. I should have talked to you in the church and not just run."

"Karlene—"

"I'll find a way to pay back your family for everything."

"Karlene, shut up!" He exhaled, his body language suddenly so weary.

She blinked away tears at his sharp tone.

He gave an exasperated sigh. "Don't cry. You did what was right."

"I'm so sorry." She choked on her tears, her voice wobbling. "I know I embarrassed you and hurt you."

"Karlene." He gripped her arms, giving her a soft shake. "Listen to me. You did what I didn't have the courage to do. We're both lucky, and you know why?"

She stared at him in confusion, her eyes suddenly dry. "Why?"

"Because you saved us from years of blandness." He released her with an amused chuckle.

"Wait. You're laughing about this?" Her heart dropped. "And blandness? I'll have you know—"

"Kar, just shut up and listen. Please."

She bit her lips together and crossed her arms.

"I appreciate your courage. Yes, of course I wish one of us had summoned some sooner." Again that rough laugh, void of amusement, and she realized he was trying. Trying to express himself after years of so much silence. "But you did the right thing by running out of that church. So, thank you."

"You didn't want to get married?" she whispered.

"It seemed like the next step."

She nodded, understanding the pressure and expectations that had led them to what hadn't truly been a bad place. But it also hadn't been the right place.

"We loved each other, but without passion." He reached out, tapped her arm. "I'll always love you. But it's more like… like you're a friend, you know? A…sister almost."

The word 'sister' hit her and she bowed her head. Would a man never see her as something more than that? As an equal or a lover?

"Know who doesn't see you as a sister?" Tom asked.

Karlene rolled her head to the side in exasperation. She really did not want him setting her up with someone right now. Her heart had been through enough this week, thank you very much.

"McCall."

Her neck snapped upright and she glared at Tom. *Joey?*

"He's more than your friend. And when he looks at you, it's the way I should have looked at you. You were right to choose him."

"I didn't choose him," she said hotly. "He just knew where I was and gave me a place to stay."

"How did he know where to find you?"

"What?"

"You bolted on Becky." He made a swooshing sound and zipped a hand through the air like a horse taking off. "Gone."

She groaned, reliving the imagined scene as he and his family realized what she'd done. "Your parents must hate me."

"They're confused and a bit hurt, but I think they're starting to understand that what you did was an act of grace and saved us all a lot of hardship down the line. Although my mom still wishes we'd walked down the aisle and given her that." He smiled, that same friendly one that was so comforting and familiar.

Karlene nodded. "Christmas must have been—"

"Kar?"

"What?"

"Go to him."

"Tom…"

"I'm serious. He's the one, Karlene. And I think he always has been."

* * *

Karlene parked her car in front of Joey's house and slowly got out, catching a roller she used for tight leg muscles. Her Ford was loaded with the mess from her apartment, the rest still at Tom's. She had today off, but would be at the arena again tomorrow to grind out knotted muscles and get her ailing players back into shape.

But today she had to figure out where she was living. And maybe figure out one other thing as well. Something bigger. A lot bigger.

Joey came across the yard, Brody at his heels, nose to the ground.

As Karlene watched Joey's face for clues about how he was feeling, she had a fleeting wish that Tom had said something to him. It would certainly make her life a lot easier, that was for sure. Although did she really want her ex playing matchmaker?

Well, maybe if her chosen match was Joey. She'd wanted that man for as long as she understood wanting someone.

She shifted awkwardly in front of him, realizing he wasn't about to sweep her into his arms and declare that she was the love and light of his life. She was going to have to do the tough stuff. She was going to have to fight for him.

Without wanting them, the tears began to flow. She swiped at them, hating herself for letting it all out. What kind of beast was she? She could run from a wedding with a dry eye, but when faced with Joey and her love for him, she cried?

Was it because he was safe? Or was it because she could lose so much if this one conversation went wrong?

She sucked in a deep breath and lifted her gaze to the man she loved. "Joey, I love you."

"I can't hear you." He pulled a rag from his back pocket. He tried to dab her eyes, but she cringed, leaning away.

"I don't know where that's been," she said.

He held her in place and tenderly wiped her wet cheeks. "Kar, would I really use a grubby rag to dry your eyes?"

She relented to his careful swipes.

Once satisfied that she was composed and dry-eyed, he stepped away. "Now, what were you saying?"

She burst into tears again. "I love you."

"Are you going to cry every time you tell me that?"

She nodded.

"Well." He seemed at a loss, his hands drifting into the back pockets of his jeans as he sized her up as though deciding what to do about her.

"I think you feel it, too," she said, swiping at her eyes, feeling a stab of impatience and frustration. "And I'm *not* on the rebound. I'm not using you. I love you and I always have."

Anger took over as he stood silently, watching her fall apart. "And you're a big, dumb-headed jerk if you can't see that! Also, our age gap doesn't matter. I'm old and mature and ready. I want ranch life and we work well together. Because we belong together. We always have. I'm only six years younger, but women mature faster, so we're even. And I don't care what my brother or anyone else thinks. I left the altar because I didn't have this." She stomped a foot and pointed at the ground between them. "I didn't *feel* this."

"That all?"

"Oh, don't tell me you don't feel it! It's something special and if you chicken out on me—"

"Kar." His patient tone insinuated that she was missing the big picture.

"I'm *not* a kid. I know my own feelings and I am in the free and clear to love you with all of my heart."

They faced off, her anger and humiliation brewing. He drew a line in the dirt with the toe of his cowboy boot, then tipped his head and watched her for a moment.

"Well? Are you going to say something?" she snapped.

His lips slowly curled into a slow smile and his eyes met hers with a warmth that filled her soul. His voice was low and relaxed and held that special tone she'd only ever heard him use with her. "It took you long enough."

"*Me*? It took *me* long enough?"

"Yeah."

"I'll have you know—"

Chuckling, he swept her into his arms, silencing her with a long awaited kissed that told her that it was all going to be okay. There was nothing held back, nothing between them. As her body pressed to his, she knew that he loved her in the way she'd always wanted and that she'd finally claimed the man she'd always desired, but had never allowed herself to be free enough to take a chance on.

And now that she was, it was going to be amazing.

* * *

* WHAT TO READ NEXT *

Check out more books by Jean Oram on the following pages. (**Hint:** If you loved the characters in this series be sure to check out the books in The Cowboys of Sweetheart Creek, Texas series. More Sweetheart Creek characters come to life! Start with THE COWBOY'S STOLEN HEART.)

Like to save on books? Buy direct from the author! Check out Jean Oram's online book shop at www.shop.jeanoram.com.

HOCKEY SWEETHEARTS

Have you read them all?

The Cupcake Cottage

Peach Blossom Hollow

Chocolate Cherry Cabin

The Peppermint Lodge

The Huckleberry Bookshop

Sugar Cookie Country House

The Gingerbread Cafe

A Tiny House Christmas

* * *

There are more stories set in Sweetheart Creek, Texas in these two series:

The Cowboys of Sweetheart Creek, Texas

The Cowboy's Stolen Heart (Levi)

The Cowboy's Secret Wish (Myles)

The Cowboy's Second Chance (Ryan)

The Cowboy's Sweet Elopement (Brant)

The Cowboy's Surprise Return (Cole)

MORE SMALL TOWN ROMANCES BY JEAN ORAM...

Veils and Vows

The Promise (Book 0: Devon & Olivia)

The Surprise Wedding (Book 1: Devon & Olivia)

A Pinch of Commitment (Book 2: Ethan & Lily)

The Wedding Plan (Book 3: Luke & Emma)

Accidentally Married (Book 4: Burke & Jill)

The Marriage Pledge (Book 5: Moe & Amy)

Mail Order Soulmate (Book 6: Zach & Catherine)

Blueberry Springs

Whiskey and Gumdrops (Mandy & Frankie)

Rum and Raindrops (Jen & Rob)

Eggnog and Candy Canes (Katie & Nash)

Sweet Treats (3 short stories—Mandy, Amber, & Nicola)

Vodka and Chocolate Drops (Amber & Scott)

Tequila and Candy Drops (Nicola & Todd)

Champagne and Lemon Drops (Beth & Oz)

The Summer Sisters

Falling for the Movie Star

Falling for the Boss

Falling for the Single Dad

Falling for the Bodyguard

Falling for the Firefighter

MORE SMALL TOWN ROMANCES BY JEAN ORAM...

Fairy Godmothers and Other Fiascos

Fairy Godmothers Aren't Cheap

Run, Run Rudolph

The Problem with Cupid

Indigo Bay

Sweet Matchmaker (Ginger and Logan)

Sweet Holiday Surprise (Cash & Alexa)

Sweet Forgiveness (Ashton & Zoe)

Sweet Troublemaker (Nick & Polly)

Sweet Joymaker (Maria & Clint)

ABOUT THE AUTHOR

Jean Oram is a *New York Times* and *USA Today* bestselling romance author. Inspiration for her small town series came from her own upbringing on the Canadian prairies. Although, so far, none of her characters have grown up in an old schoolhouse or worked on a bee farm. Jean still lives on the prairie with her husband, two kids, and big shaggy dog where she can be found out playing in the snow or hiking.

Become an Official Fan:
www.facebook.com/groups/jeanoramfans
Instagram: www.instagram.com/author_jeanoram
Facebook: www.facebook.com/JeanOramAuthor
Shop: shop.jeanoram.com
Newsletter: www.jeanoram.com/signup
Website & blog: www.jeanoram.com